BEARS IN THE NIGHT

by Stan and Jan Berenstain

A Bright & Early Book

RANDOM HOUSE / NEW YORK

In bed

Out of bed

Out of bed

To the window

At the window

Out the window

Out the window

Down the tree

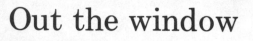

Out the window

Down the tree

Over the wall

Over the wall

Under the bridge

Under the bridge

Around the lake

Under the bridge

Around the lake

Between the rocks

Through the woods

Out the window

Down the tree

Over the wall

Under the bridge

Around the lake

Between the rocks

Through the woods

Up
Spook
Hill!

Down Spook Hill
Through the woods
Between the rocks
Around the lake
Under the bridge
Over the wall
Up the tree . . .

In the window!

Back in bed